IN THE
DINOSAUR'S PAW

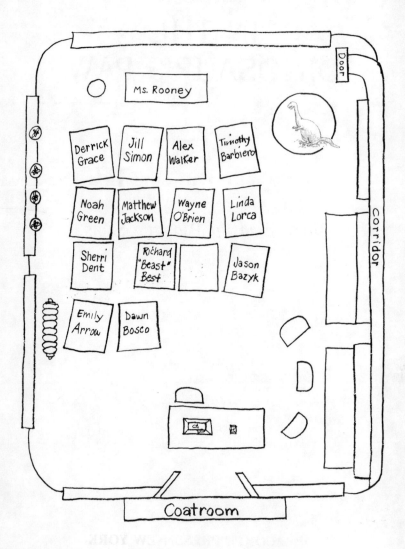

Ms. Rooney

| Derrick Grace | Jill Simon | Alex Walker | Timothy Barbiero |

| Noah Green | Matthew Jackson | Wayne O'Brien | Linda Lorca |

| Sherri Dent | Richard "Beast" Best | | Jason Bazyk |

| Emily Arrow | Dawn Bosco |

Door

Corridor

Coatroom

IN THE DINOSAUR'S PAW

Patricia Reilly Giff

Illustrated by Blanche Sims

E.G. Sherburne School

DELACORTE PRESS/NEW YORK

Published by
Delacorte Press
1 Dag Hammarskjold Plaza
New York, N.Y. 10017

This work was first published as a Dell Yearling Book.

Manufactured in the United States of America

First printing

Library of Congress Cataloging in Publication Data

Giff, Patricia Reilly.
In the dinosaur's paw.

(The Kids of the Polk Street School; no. 5)
Summary: When the kids in Ms. Rooney's class
return to school after Christmas, one of them suspects
he has found a magic ruler that makes wishes come true.
[1. Schools—Fiction] I. Sims, Blanche, ill. II. Title.
III. Series: Kids of the Polk Street School; no. 5.
PZ7.G3626In 1986   [E]
ISBN 0-385-29496-4
Library of Congress Catalog Card Number: 85-32541

To Joan Hanson

IN THE
DINOSAUR'S PAW

Chapter 1

Richard Best hid his green mittens under the bed.

Baby Christmas mittens.

He'd never wear them. Especially not to school.

Then he remembered. He needed a ruler today.

He looked under the bed again. He threw everything out of the floor of his closet.

"Hurry up, Richard," his sister, Holly, screamed from downstairs.

His mother poked her head into his room. "This room is the worst," she said. "I'm glad you're going back to school."

Richard pulled out his dresser drawer. "I have to have a ruler," he said.

"Why didn't you look for that on Saturday?" his mother asked. "Or the day after Christmas?"

"First day back is dinosaurs," Richard said. "Ms. Rooney says we can't do dinosaurs without a ruler."

"Richard," Holly yelled again.

His mother looked under his bed. "No ruler," she said. "But I found your nice green mittens." She pulled them out. "Here."

"I think it's late," Richard said. He took the mittens. Then he tore down the stairs.

Holly was waiting at the door.

"You make me late," she said. "Every day."

"Go without me," Richard said. He went into the kitchen.

He grabbed his lunch bag.

He sniffed it a little. Tuna fish again.

Horrible.

He banged out the door in back of Holly. They started for the Polk Street School.

Some winter this was, he thought. No snow.

Not one drop over the Christmas vacation.

If only it would snow.

If only he had a ruler.

"Hurry," Holly said. She started to walk faster.

Richard walked slower.

He hated to walk to school with Holly.

As soon as they crossed Linden Avenue he stopped. He stood in front of the A&P store until Holly was gone.

There was a white mountain in the A&P store window.

It was made of toilet paper rolls.

Richard walked to the corner to wait for Emily. They were going to walk together every day now.

He didn't want people to see him standing in front of a toilet paper mountain.

He thought about school today. Maybe Ms. Rooney wouldn't let him do dinosaurs without a ruler.

He wondered how you did dinosaurs anyway.

Ms. Rooney hadn't told them that yet. She'd just said, "Don't forget to bring a ruler. After vacation we'll do dinosaurs."

"Hey, Beast," a voice yelled.

It was Emily Arrow. She was walking with Jill Simon.

Emily held up a red and green purse. "This is one of my presents."

"Want to trade lunches?" Richard asked.

Emily raised her shoulders up in the air. "I have cheese. The orange shiny kind."

Richard made a face. "No, thanks," he said.

"I'm not trading," Jill said. "I have peanut butter."

They turned the corner. Richard looked at the house with the white fence. "I think that dog is outside."

Jill shivered.

The dog began to bark. They started to run.

They stopped at the corner. Richard tried to catch his breath. "Ruff-a-roo," he yelled back at the dog.

"Someday that dog might get out," Jill said.

Emily laughed. "Don't worry. We're fast."

"Do you have an extra ruler?" Richard asked.

"I was just going to ask you that," Emily said.

"Hey." Jill pointed to the other side of the street. Someone was hopping over a garbage can cover.

"Look at that grasshopper," Emily said.

Richard laughed.

"What are you laughing at?" the boy yelled.

It was Drake Evans.

"Isn't that the kid who was in your class?" Emily asked. "Before you were left back?"

Richard nodded a little. He didn't like to think about being left back.

"Ruff-a-roo," he yelled at Drake.

Drake started across the street toward them.

He had a mean look on his face.

"Yikes," yelled Emily. "Let's go."

They raced down the street toward school.

Richard looked over his shoulder.

Drake was running after them.

"I'm going to get you, Richard," he yelled.

They turned the last corner.

Up ahead was the Polk Street School. Ms. Rooney was standing in front.

"Whew," Emily said.

They slowed down. In back of them Drake slowed down too.

"Ruff-a-roo," Richard said.

"Hi, Ms. Rooney," Emily said.

"It's going to be a great day," said Ms. Rooney. "I hope you remembered your rulers."

"Did you have a nice vacation?" Richard asked Ms. Rooney.

"Super," she said.

They went into Room 113. Maybe his ruler was in his desk, Richard thought.

While he was looking his friend Matthew Jackson slid into the seat in front of him.

Richard took a breath.

Matthew had the wet-the-bed smell.

"I have a new ruler," Matthew said. "It's for the dinosaurs."

Richard shoved his hand into his desk. There were piles of papers. He didn't feel a ruler.

He went into the coatroom. He dropped his mittens on the floor. He put his lunch on the shelf.

He wished it were Christmas again.

He wished he had a ruler.

Chapter 2

Ms. Rooney was drawing on the blackboard.

Richard was starving.

Too bad his lunch was in the coatroom.

Ms. Rooney stood back. She looked at her drawing. "Not too good," she said.

She began to erase part of it.

Richard fished way back in his desk for something to eat. Maybe there was a piece of candy left over from before the winter vacation.

His hand closed on something. A ruler.

He couldn't believe it.

It looked a little like his old ruler.

But not exactly.

"Guess what this is," Ms. Rooney said.

"It looks like a giraffe," Richard said. "But I think it's a dinosaur."

"Right," said Ms. Rooney. "But it's not supposed to look like a giraffe." She erased the dinosaur's neck.

Richard turned the ruler over. On the back there were big red crayon initials. *D.T.*

He looked around. There was no *D.T.* in the room.

They had a Dawn Bosco and a Derrick Grace.

"Yes," said Ms. Rooney. "This is a picture of the fiercest dinosaur. His name was Tyrannosaurus rex."

Crazy name, Richard thought. He began to rub the red *D.T.* off his new ruler.

"We're going to pretend," said Ms. Rooney. "We'll make believe that Tyrannosaurus lives in the hall."

Richard closed his eyes. He could see the big dinosaur.

He was green. He had black spots.

He had a long purple stripe on his tail.

Matthew turned around. He pulled his lips back.

All his teeth showed.

"Grr," he said to Richard. "I'm one of those Ty-Tyranno-what-you-call-its."

"Ruff-a-roo," Richard said.

"All right, class," said Ms. Rooney. "Pick up your rulers and line up."

Emily waved her hand around in the air.

So did Jill Simon.

Ms. Rooney sighed. "Don't tell me," she said.

"I forgot—" Emily began.

"Your ruler," said Ms. Rooney. "You too, Jill?"

Jill looked down at her desk. "Yes."

Ms. Rooney reached into her desk. She pulled out two rulers. "Anybody else?"

Dawn Bosco raised her hand.

"Some people are going to be in trouble," Ms. Rooney said, "if they don't start to remember."

Ms. Rooney fished in her desk again. She gave Dawn another ruler. "Let's go," she said.

Outside in the hall Richard waved his ruler around. He banged it against Matthew's.

Matthew banged back.

Richard tapped the ruler on Matthew's head. "Got you," he whispered.

"Argg," Matthew said. "I'm dead."

"What's going on at the end of the line?" Ms. Rooney asked.

Everyone was quiet.

"Now," said Ms. Rooney. "Just close your eyes. Make believe it's hot. Steamy. You're in a swamp."

"What's a—" Jill Simon began.

"A swamp," Ms. Rooney said. "That's a wet, marshy place. A place with snakes and crocodiles."

Richard closed his eyes.

"There are dinosaur birds flying overhead," said Ms. Rooney.

Richard could almost hear their leathery wings.

"Par, par, par," Matthew whispered. "They're flying straight toward—"

"On the ground," said Ms. Rooney, "many dinosaurs are eating huge plants."

11

"Crunch, crunch," said Matthew.

Ms. Rooney stared at Richard and Matthew.

Richard took a step away from Matthew.

"And then there was Tyrannosaurus," said Ms. Rooney. "He was the king. A terrible king."

Richard shivered a little.

"He had teeth like knives," said Ms. Rooney.

"Are you sure there are none left?" Jill asked.

"They died millions of years ago," Ms. Rooney said.

"Whew," said Emily Arrow. "I was getting worried."

Ms. Rooney pointed to the ceiling. "Tyrannosaurus would take up two floors of our school."

Richard could see the dinosaur's head.

It was poking up into the sixth-grade classroom.

Mrs. Kettle was screaming. Mean Mrs. Kettle.

It served her right.

Tyrannosaurus opened his mouth.

Next to Richard, Matthew giggled.

"Too bad there isn't one of those things left," he whispered. "He could grab Mrs. Kettle."

Richard smiled. "Just what I was thinking."

Ms. Rooney frowned. "Is someone talking?"

Richard took another step away from Matthew.

"Ty was about forty-five feet long," said Ms. Rooney. "That's from his head to the tip of his tail." She looked around. "How can we find out how much space he'd use?"

Noah Green raised his hand. So did Dawn Bosco.

Richard ducked down. He hoped Ms. Rooney wouldn't call on him.

"Noah," said Ms. Rooney.

Noah put his ruler up in the air. "My ruler is one foot long."

"You're on the right track," said Ms. Rooney.

Matthew leaned over. "Noah's always on the right track."

"*Vroom, vroom,*" said Richard.

"If you put your ruler on the floor," said Noah, "and move it forty-five times . . ."

"I was going to say that too," said Emily.

"That's how long he'd be," said Noah.

13

"Good thinking," said Ms. Rooney.

Richard looked down at the floor. He didn't know what they were talking about.

"Start at the end of the hall," Ms. Rooney said. "Move your ruler forty-five times. That's how long Ty is."

"Simple," said Matthew.

"Simple," Richard said. He waited to see what everyone was going to do.

Emily knelt on the floor. She put her ruler down.

Then she put her finger at the end of the ruler. She moved the ruler.

"Oh," said Richard. He began to move his ruler along too. "One," he whispered to himself. "Two. Three."

After a while he forgot what number he was up to.

He made believe he was counting. "Twenty-one."

He looked out the hall window. It was snowing.

In front of him Noah yelled, "Forty-five."

14

Everyone stopped and looked at Noah.

They looked back to where they had started.

"Wow," said Emily.

"That guy must have been a giant," Richard said.

He followed everyone back into the classroom.

He took out a piece of paper.

He drew a dinosaur. A green one with a bunch of black spots. It had a purple stripe down its tail.

"This is my lucky day," he told Matthew. "I wished for a ruler and I found one. I wished for snow. And look out the window."

"Snow," Matthew said. "This is my lucky day too."

Then he pointed to Richard's ruler. "I just thought of something."

"What?" Richard asked.

"*D.T.*," Matthew said. "Dinosaur. Tyrannosaurus whatever-you-call-it. Ty."

Richard looked down at his ruler.

He could still see the red crayon mark. *D.T.*

16

"Do you think maybe a dinosaur ghost . . ." Matthew said.

"Don't be silly," Richard said. He put the ruler back into his desk.

He looked down at his drawing. It looked as if the dinosaur were smiling at him.

Chapter 3

It was almost time to go home.

Richard wondered how deep the snow was.

The pencil sharpener was next to the window.

He grabbed his pencil. He hurried across the room.

"Richard," Ms. Rooney began. "How many times—"

Just then the door opened.

It was Mrs. Gates, Drake Evans's teacher. "I just had a wonderful idea," she told Ms. Rooney.

Richard stuck his pencil in the sharpener. He stood on tiptoe to look at the snow.

He could hear Ms. Rooney and Mrs. Gates talking.

He pushed open the window a little.

There was a thick coat of snow on the window-sill.

Maybe there was enough for a snowball.

He'd scoop it up and carry it back to his desk.

He looked back over his shoulder.

Ms. Rooney and Mrs. Gates were standing at the door.

He grabbed a mound of snow. It was freezing cold.

He raced back to his seat.

Matthew was doing his math workbook.

Richard leaned forward. He put the snowball against Matthew's neck.

"Yeow," Matthew yelled.

Richard dropped the snowball.

Ms. Rooney jumped. "I can't believe my ears," she told Mrs. Gates.

"I can't either," said Mrs. Gates. "I hope they calm down before they get to my class."

Mrs. Gates went out to the hall.

Ms. Rooney closed the door. "Disgraceful," she said. "We can't even have a visitor in this room."

She looked around. "Who was that?"

Nobody answered.

Richard rubbed his hands on his jeans.

He could see the snowball on the floor.

It was starting to melt a little. But not much.

Suppose Ms. Rooney saw it.

"Who made that noise?" Ms. Rooney asked again.

Matthew leaned over his workbook. "Nine and four," he said. "Twelve. No, eleven."

"I'm glad to see Matthew Jackson is working," Ms. Rooney said. "Some people are very good workers. It's too bad that a few people spoil everything."

Richard looked down at the snowball.

He wished it would melt faster. A lot faster.

"Mrs. Gates had such a lovely surprise for us," Ms. Rooney said.

Maybe he should put something on top of the snowball. A book.

He reached into his desk. He could feel his reader.

Ms. Rooney would be mad if his reader got wet.

"We are going on a trip," said Ms. Rooney.

He could feel the ruler in the back of his desk.

The *D.T.* ruler. The dinosaur ruler.

He pulled it out.

"Our class will go with Mrs. Gates's class," said Ms. Rooney.

Richard pointed the ruler at the snowball.

If only it were a dinosaur ruler.

It would grant all his wishes.

It would melt the snowball in two seconds.

He looked down at the snowball.

It was melting. It was really melting fast.

"We are going to see a dinosaur," said Ms. Rooney. "On Friday."

"In a zoo?" Emily asked. "I thought there weren't any."

Ms. Rooney shook her head. "Not a live one. We're going to a museum."

Matthew looked back at Richard. "Yucks," he said. "I knew it was going to be something like a museum."

22

"I knew it too," Richard said. He was still watching the snowball.

Only a sliver of white was left.

Richard looked at his ruler.

It wasn't a dinosaur ruler.

Only babies could believe that.

But all his wishes were coming true.

He'd have to tell Matthew.

"Yes," said Ms. Rooney. "There is a big dinosaur in the museum. His bones were found. Someone put them together. You'll get an idea of what he was really like."

Emily Arrow leaned forward. "Beast," she whispered. She looked worried.

"Time to get your jackets," Ms. Rooney said.

Emily's row stood up first. "It's going to be a terrible trip," she whispered as she went past.

Richard sneaked into the closet. He looked around for his green mittens.

"We'll have to spend the whole day getting away from Drake," Emily said.

His mittens were under Dawn's schoolbag.

"You're right, Emily," he said.

He went back to his seat.

Too bad his ruler wasn't really a dinosaur ruler.

He'd wish for something to happen.

Especially to Drake Evans.

Chapter 4

Richard pulled out his homework pad. It said:

Go to L.
Find out 5 things about D.
Write 3X:
        dinosaur
        Tyrannosaurus

He sighed.

He had made a great fort in the snow this afternoon.

He had forgotten all about the library.

He went upstairs. He took off his socks. They were soaking wet.

He was going to be in trouble tomorrow. He wouldn't be able to do part of his homework. The five dinosaur things part.

Ms. Rooney was going to be mad as anything.

"Can I borrow some looseleaf?" he yelled to Holly.

"Don't you ever have anything?" she shouted back.

"I just need one piece," he said.

"Get your own," she yelled.

He couldn't find any more socks. He went downstairs again.

"Are these your mittens on the floor?" his mother asked.

Richard felt like saying no. He felt like saying they belonged to a dinosaur.

He felt like telling Holly that a dinosaur was going to get her.

He picked up his wet mittens. They had a funny wool smell.

He threw them in the hall closet. Then he went out to the kitchen.

Holly was sitting at the table. Her papers were spread out all over the place.

"Do you have to take up the whole world?" he asked.

26

Holly made a face at him. She gave him two pieces of looseleaf. They were wrinkled.

He wrote *dinosaur* three times.

Then he wrote *Ty* —

He had forgotten his heading.

He crumpled up the first piece of looseleaf.

He started on the second.

Under the heading he wrote *dinosaur* three times again.

Then he wrote *Tyrannosourrus.*

Wrong. *Tyrranosaurus.*

"Can I borrow an eraser?" he asked Holly.

She slid her pink eraser across the table.

He erased the last part of the word.

There was a round dark spot from the eraser.

Ms. Rooney didn't like it when he had marks all over his homework.

He thought about asking Holly for more paper.

"How about—" he began.

"No," she said.

He finished his spelling. Then he drew a fat black line underneath with his dinosaur ruler.

If only the library were still open, he could find out five things about dinosaurs.

"Do you know a thing about dinosaurs?" he asked Holly.

"Keep quiet," Holly said. "They lay eggs."

"That's chickens," Richard said. "Don't you know anything?"

"Dinosaurs do so lay eggs," Holly said.

Richard looked at her.

He wondered if she was telling the truth.

He stood up and went over to the window. He could see his fort outside.

It was the best fort he had ever made.

Drake Evans was walking all over the top of it.

"Hey," he yelled. He knocked on the window as hard as he could. "Get off there."

Drake stamped hard on the top of the fort.

"Hey," Richard said. He ran upstairs to his bedroom. He pulled his jacket off the hook.

"I'm going to get you, Drake," he whispered.

He ran downstairs again.

He looked out the window. Maybe Drake would be gone by now.

Drake was sitting there on top of the fort.

"How soon is supper?" Richard yelled to his mother.

"Ten minutes," she called back.

Richard opened the front door a crack. "Get off my fort," he yelled.

"Make me," Drake shouted.

"I would," Richard said. "But I have to have supper in a minute."

"It's freezing in here," Holly screamed.

Richard slammed the door shut.

He thought about asking his mother for some dinosaur things.

But she had gone down to the laundry room.

She probably didn't know about dinosaurs anyway.

He went upstairs to look out his bedroom window.

Drake was still sitting on the fort.

It was almost dark. He'd probably get sick.

Richard hoped he would get sick.

He hoped Drake would get so sick, he wouldn't be able to go on the trip to the museum on Friday.

Chapter 5

Richard watched Holly eat her cereal.

She was taking a long time. Good.

He took a huge bite of his toast and stood up.

"I'm ready for school," he said. "I'd better not wait for Holly."

His mother frowned. "I don't want you to cross Linden Avenue by yourself."

Richard stamped upstairs to his room.

His mother thought he was a big baby.

"Cars whizzing all over the place," his mother called after him. "And you never look both ways."

"I don't want to walk to school with that dummy," Holly said.

"You're the dummy," Richard shouted back.

He sat on the floor. He pulled on his boots.

Everything was going wrong.

His homework. The looseleaf.

Then he remembered. Worst of all. The class trip. The trip with Drake Evans.

He picked his dinosaur ruler up off the floor.

If only he could think of five dinosaur things.

He closed his eyes. He rubbed the ruler.

Suddenly a dinosaur thing popped into his head.

Dinosaurs lived millions of years ago.

Of course. What else?

They lived in swampy places.

Easy. Why hadn't he thought of that last night?

He ran downstairs.

"Could I have one more piece of looseleaf?" he asked.

Holly wiped her mouth. "No."

"How come I never have looseleaf?" Richard asked his mother. "How come Holly has everything?"

"Because you keep making mistakes," Holly said. "Because you keep wrecking up your paper."

"Give him one piece," his mother said. "Please."

Holly yanked a piece of looseleaf out of her book.

Richard took it and knelt on the floor.

Quickly he began to write:

Dinosaurs lived millyons of yeers ago.
Dinosaurs lived in sooamps.

He ran upstairs to get his ruler.

On the way downstairs he remembered two more things:

They were as big as a school.
They ate grass.

"I'm ready," Holly said. "Let's go."

"I'm not ready," Richard said. "Go alone."

Quickly he wrote:

They ate each other.

Holly leaned over. "Are you going to give that mess to Ms. Rooney?" She started to laugh.

35

Richard looked down at his paper.

He should have put a book underneath his paper.

The pencil had gone through the paper, right into the rug.

The paper had about four holes in it.

He stood up. So what?

He had five good things about dinosaurs.

Ms. Rooney would love it.

He grabbed his schoolbag. He put his homework and his ruler inside.

Then he put on his jacket and mittens.

He followed Holly out the door.

He thought about the five dinosaur things. They had popped right into his head.

Maybe it was because of the *D.T.* ruler.

"Come on, slowpoke," Holly called. She was walking fast.

Richard walked as slow as he could.

He saw Holly look back. She was watching him cross Linden Avenue.

Then she turned the corner.

Richard looked in the A&P store window.

They must have changed it last night. Now about a zillion cans were stacked up in front.

Soup cans. Pea soup cans.

Yuck.

Then he saw Emily Arrow and Jill Simon.

Emily picked up a scoop of snow with her mittens.

She licked the top of the snow.

"It tastes like my mitten," she said.

Jill looked down the street. "We could go the long way," she said. "We wouldn't have to pass the dog."

"It's late," Emily said. "We can run right past him."

Jill looked as if she were going to cry.

Richard thought about the *D.T.* ruler. "Don't worry."

"The dog moved away?" Emily asked.

Richard shook his head. "No. I'm going to wish the dog's not outside."

"Don't be silly," Emily said.

"You'll see," Richard told her.

They hurried down the block. They didn't see the dog.

"I told you," Richard said.

He was glad he had the *D.T.* ruler.

He was going to keep it forever.

Chapter 6

"Today is National Handwriting Day," said Ms. Rooney. "Does anyone know what that means?"

Richard slid down in his seat.

Too bad Matthew wasn't in school. His desk was empty. There was a big open spot in front of Richard.

Ms. Rooney could see him easily.

"National Handwriting Day," said Ms. Rooney again.

Richard looked around.

Nobody knew what Ms. Rooney was talking about.

"I'll give you a hint," said Ms. Rooney. "*Nation* means *country*."

Timothy Barbiero's hand shot up. "I know," he said. "Everyone in the country has to think about handwriting."

"Very good, Timothy," said Ms. Rooney.

The door opened.

It was Matthew. He was covered with snow.

Ms. Rooney looked at him. "I see we have a snowman in Room 113," she said.

Matthew pulled off his blue hat. He shook it. Little lumps of snow dropped onto the floor.

"It's a little late," said Ms. Rooney.

"I know," said Matthew. "I fell."

Richard sat up straight. He was glad Matthew wasn't absent. He wanted to tell Matthew about his five dinosaur things. And his *D.T.* ruler.

"Matthew," he whispered in a loud voice.

But Matthew went to the coatroom.

"Don't put your wet stuff near mine," Dawn called.

"How about putting your coat on the radiator?" Ms. Rooney said. "It will dry off a little."

Matthew threw his coat on top of the radiator. Then he sat down.

"What was I talking about?" asked Ms. Rooney.

Richard gave Matthew a tap. "I was waiting for you."

"I had a bad thing happen," Matthew said. "Drake—"

"Don't worry," Richard said. "I think nothing bad is going to happen anymore."

Matthew turned around. "That's good. How come?"

"Let's settle down," Ms. Rooney said.

Richard leaned forward.

He wanted to tell Matthew that all his wishes were coming true.

"Listen, Matthew," he said.

"Listen, Richard," Ms. Rooney said. "Let's get down to business."

Emily Arrow put her hand up. "We were talking about handwriting."

"Right," said Ms. Rooney. "Today we'll try hard. We'll have the best handwriting in the Polk Street School."

Richard thought about his homework.

Holly was right. It was a mess.

Maybe he should wish that it were neater.

Maybe he should wish that it were the neatest in the class.

Maybe he should wish that it were the neatest in the whole country.

He looked out the window.

It wouldn't be fair to wish about his homework. Besides, it might not work.

"Well, then," said Ms. Rooney. "Make your handwriting the best today." She smiled at Richard.

Everyone started to copy the boardwork.

It was a letter.

Dear Mother,
    On Friday we are going on a trip. We'll take a bus. We'll see a dinosaur.
    Please send your child with a bag lunch.
                    Love,

                    _____

Dawn Bosco leaned forward. "You're not supposed to write the line," she said. "You have to put your name in there."

43

Carefully Richard wrote *Richard Best* on top of the line.

Then he read his note again.

He hoped his mother didn't think he was going to see a live dinosaur. Maybe she would be worried.

He thought for a moment. Then he wrote:

P.S. The dinosaur is dead.

He tapped Matthew on the shoulder.

Matthew turned around. He looked cold.

"My socks are all wet," he said.

"I have exciting news," said Richard.

"I have terrible news," said Matthew. "My homework is all wet."

"Will you be quiet?" Sherri Dent said.

"Yes," said Ms. Rooney. "Everyone should be quiet."

Richard looked down at his boardwork.

He wondered how soon he'd get a chance to talk to Matthew. He hoped recess would come soon.

Chapter 7

It was time for special-help reading.

Richard, Emily, Alex Walker, and Matthew raced down the hall.

Mrs. Paris was waiting. "I hear you're going on a dinosaur trip," she said.

"Right," said Emily. "We're going to see dinosaur bones. They're stuck together to make a dinosaur."

Richard didn't want to think about the trip.

He didn't want to think about Drake Evans.

"Mrs. Gates's class is going too," Alex told Mrs. Paris.

Richard looked at the new story in his reader.

On top was a picture of a king.

There was a girl too.

It looked as if she were made of gold.

Mrs. Paris sat down at the table with them. "Have you ever heard of King Midas?" she asked.

Everyone shook his head.

"Well," said Mrs. Paris, "you're in for a treat. Here's a story you can zip right into."

"He had a crazy name," Emily said.

"Richard has a crazy nickname," Matthew said. "Beast."

Richard made a beast face.

Mrs. Paris smiled. "I'd hate to tell you what my first name is."

"What?" Emily asked.

"I'll never tell," said Mrs. Paris.

"Dawn must have a terrible middle name," Emily said. "She won't tell anyone what it is."

Emily narrowed her eyes. "She *said* it was Tiffanie. But it really begins with an *M*."

"Probably Mabel," Alex said.

"Mabel Cable," Matthew said.

Mrs. Paris tapped the King Midas book. "Maybe we should get to reading."

It was Richard's turn to read first.

Mrs. Paris was right. It was an easy book.

46

It was about a king who loved gold. First he turned his flowers into gold. He turned his socks into gold. Then he even turned his daughter into gold.

Richard thought about the trip.

Drake was going to get him.

Richard looked across the table. Matthew was still a little wet.

Drake Evans had probably pushed him.

If only Drake weren't going on the trip.

If only Drake would move before Friday.

"Wake up, Richard," said Mrs. Paris.

Richard jumped.

Mrs. Paris smiled at him. "Do you think the king was happy?" she asked.

"King Midas?" Richard asked.

Mrs. Paris nodded.

"Beast was asleep, all right," said Emily.

"I think he was happy," Richard said. "I'd love to have a bunch of gold."

"That's wrong," said Matthew.

Richard looked down at his book.

"He turned his daughter into gold," Emily said. "She couldn't even move."

"Oh," Richard said.

"And how would you like to wear gold socks?" Matthew asked. "You couldn't even wiggle your toes."

"I guess you'd get blisters," Richard said.

He wished Drake had blisters. Big fat blisters.

Right on his two fat feet.

Then he wouldn't be able to get his boots on.

He'd have to stay home from the trip.

"Yes," said Mrs. Paris. "I guess the king became sad about turning everything into gold."

"Well," said Richard. "It's too bad he couldn't turn just a few things into gold."

Mrs. Paris laughed.

They closed their books. Then they drew pictures of the story.

Emily drew King Midas.

Matthew drew a gold sock.

Matthew wasn't such a good artist, Richard thought.

His sock looked like a yellow box. A box with a tail on the end.

Richard drew a dinosaur. It was even bigger than the one he had made the other day.

It had more black spots.

It had fire coming from its mouth.

Emily tapped him on the shoulder. "This picture is supposed to be about King Midas."

"I forgot," Richard said.

"It's a good dinosaur," said Mrs. Paris.

"What's that in his paw?" Matthew asked.

"I don't think dinosaurs had paws," Alex said.

"It's a ruler," Richard said.

Matthew grinned. "I know why."

The bell rang. It was time to go back to Ms. Rooney's room.

They stood up. "Come on, Mrs. Paris," Emily said. "Tell us your first name."

Mrs. Paris laughed. "Never."

"What does it begin with?" Richard asked.

"*M,*" said Mrs. Paris. "And it's worse than Mabel."

In the hall Richard and Matthew stopped for a drink.

"What's your exciting news?" Matthew asked.

"It's about the *D.T.* ruler," Richard said. "All my wishes are coming true."

"Wow," said Matthew. "Just like King Midas."

Richard counted. "First I found the ruler. Then there was the snow wish, and the homework wish, and the dog wish—" He broke off. "Not like King Midas."

"How about a million-dollar wish?" Matthew asked.

Ms. Rooney poked her head out of Room 113. "Alex and Emily were back ahead of you."

Richard and Matthew hurried into the classroom.

Richard started his math work. He wrote the numbers slowly and carefully.

It was National Handwriting Day.

He wanted his numbers to look perfect.

Maybe he should wish for a million dollars.

No, that would be greedy, Richard thought.

Just like King Midas.

The only thing he really wanted right now was for Drake Evans to go away.

Chapter 8

"We have to rush this afternoon," said Ms. Rooney on Thursday. "Tomorrow is the trip. We have to finish all our work."

Richard's pencil point was broken.

He rushed to the pencil sharpener.

"We don't have time for that," said Ms. Rooney.

Richard sat down again.

"I have an extra pencil," Matthew said.

Richard took the pencil. "You saved my life," he told Matthew.

He opened his notebook.

He had to copy five sentences. He had to put in the capitals and the periods.

He was glad it wasn't National Handwriting Day anymore.

Matthew's pencil was a wreck.

It made his heading look sloppy.

Emily walked past on her way to the wastebasket.

"Hey, guys," she whispered. "Let's try to find out Mrs. Paris's name."

"With an *M*?" Matthew asked. "My mother's name is Molly."

"My mother's name is Lisa," said Richard.

"Lisa," Emily said. "That's not an *M*."

Ms. Rooney tapped her hand on her desk.

Richard wrote the first sentence.

tomorrow is trip day

He erased the *t* in *tomorrow*. He made a big *T*. Then he put a dot after *day*. Perfect.

"Guess what?" Matthew said.

Richard leaned forward. "What?"

"I don't think Drake is going on the trip," Matthew said.

Richard reached into his desk. He gave his ruler a pat.

"Drake moved?" he asked.

Ms. Rooney walked down the aisle.

She looked at Richard's notebook.

"Nice work," she said. "But you should have finished a lot more."

Quickly Richard wrote the next sentence.

we are going on a bus

Ms. Rooney tapped his paper. "What about the *W*?"

"I was just going to make it a big one," he said.

Ms. Rooney went to the other side of the room.

"Drake is sick," Matthew said.

Richard put a dot after *bus*. "Sick?" he asked.

"Very sick."

"I wished for him to move away," he told Matthew.

Matthew turned around again. "Maybe it's because he got wet in the snow."

"Playing on my fort," Richard said.

Matthew shook his head. "No, helping me out of the snow when I fell."

The door opened. It was Mrs. Gates.

Suddenly Richard remembered. He had made lots of Drake wishes. Terrible Drake wishes.

He had wished Drake would disappear.

He had wished Drake would get sick.

He had even wished that Drake would get blisters.

"Drake must have gotten wet in the snow," Richard said.

"I was stuck," Matthew said.

Mrs. Gates said hello to Ms. Rooney. "Is Matthew Jackson here?" she asked.

"He certainly is," said Ms. Rooney.

"You live on Drake's street, don't you?" Mrs. Gates asked Matthew.

"Three doors away," Matthew said.

"Good," said Mrs. Gates. "Will you take his homework to him?"

Mrs. Gates looked at Ms. Rooney. "Drake can't afford to miss one minute of work."

"I hope he'll make the trip," Ms. Rooney said.

Mrs. Gates looked sad for a minute. "He's really been looking forward to it."

Richard started his next sentence.

we will have a great time

"I think you made a bad wish," Matthew whispered. "Maybe something is going to happen to Drake."

Richard put his pencil down. "Do you think it's my fault?"

"Don't worry," Matthew said. "I won't tell the police."

Richard swallowed.

Matthew went to the front of the room.

He took Drake's reading workbook and his notebook.

"Don't drop them in the snow," Mrs. Gates said. "Tell Drake I hope he's feeling better."

Richard put a dot at the end of the sentence.

He hoped nothing was going to happen to Drake.

Nothing terrible. Suppose . . .

Matthew sat down again. "I don't know why Mrs. Gates is sending this stuff home," he said. "Drake may not need it anymore."

"What do you mean?" Richard asked. Then he sighed. He knew what Matthew meant.

Richard finished his sentences.

He went to the coatroom. He put on his mittens.

"No homework," said Ms. Rooney.

Richard walked outside with Matthew and Emily.

"Maybe Mrs. Paris's name is Milly," said Emily.

"Milly, Tilly, Silly," said Matthew.

Emily and Matthew laughed. But Richard didn't laugh. He was thinking about Drake Evans.

He sat on the steps to wait for Holly.

Suddenly he knew what he could do about Drake.

He ran back to the classroom.

He hoped the door wouldn't be locked.

Chapter 9

Richard raced down the hall.

Holly was coming out of her room. "Let's go."

"I have to get something," Richard said.

"He never remembers anything," Holly said to her friend Joanne.

Richard turned the knob of Room 113.

Ms. Rooney was still inside.

So was Dawn Bosco. She was washing the blackboard.

"Your books were all over the floor," said Ms. Rooney.

"Sorry," Richard said. He went back to his desk.

Ms. Rooney had picked up all his books.

They were on the desk in a neat pile.

"Time to go," Ms. Rooney told Dawn.

Richard looked in his desk. He didn't see his *D.T.* ruler.

He pulled everything out of the desk.

It was gone.

He had to find it.

He had to make a *D.T.* wish. A good wish for Drake Evans.

"Good-bye, Ms. Rooney," said Dawn. She waved at Richard.

"Hurry, Richard," said Ms. Rooney.

"I can't find my—" Richard began.

"Trip tomorrow," said Ms. Rooney. "You don't need anything."

Richard went back down the hall.

Holly was outside. "Thanks a lot, Richard," she said. "You almost made us freeze to death."

He followed them down the street.

As soon as they crossed Linden Avenue he stopped to look in the A&P store window.

It was just the same. A bunch of pea soup cans.

He caught up with Jill and Emily.

"You were right," Jill told him. "That dog hasn't been out for two days."

Emily smiled. "Beast has powerful wishes, I guess."

"Not anymore," Richard said.

Jill looked a little worried. "Do you think the dog is going to be outside?"

"Maybe." Richard wondered if he'd ever see the ruler again. He scooped up some snow. He threw it at a tree.

"Yes," he told Jill. "I think that dog will be out there."

Jill shivered. "I guess I'm going the long way."

"You have to be brave," Emily said.

"That's right," said Richard.

They started down the street.

He hoped Drake was brave. Poor mean, fat Drake.

Sometimes he was a little mean to Drake too.

"There's the fence," Jill said.

62

They slowed down a little.

"Do you see the dog?" Jill asked.

Richard shook his head.

"See," said Emily. "Richard's wishes are still powerful."

Richard looked at the fence. Maybe Emily was right. Maybe he could make wishes even though the ruler was gone.

He wished that Drake would be all right.

He wished that he wouldn't move away.

He wished that he weren't sick.

He even wished that he didn't have blisters.

Then he made a wish for Jill.

He wished that the dog would be inside the house.

"All right," said Jill. "I'm being brave."

They walked toward the house with the fence.

Suddenly the dog began to bark.

He jumped up against the fence.

The three of them stopped.

"Yikes," said Emily.

They rushed back down the block.

They started for home the long way.

"I guess my power is gone," Richard said.

Chapter 10

Today was the trip. On the way to school Richard looked for Emily and Jill.

They were nowhere in sight. Maybe they had gone on ahead.

In the hall he stopped under the painting of James K. Polk.

He opened his brown paper bag lunch.

His mother had made him a special trip lunch. Peanut butter and jelly. Two chocolate chip cookies. A banana. A small can of grape drink.

All his favorites.

Slowly he walked down the hall to Room 113.

Everyone was running around.

Wayne O'Brien was feeding the fish.

Alex was watering the plants.

Matthew was sitting on the floor. He was eating a cookie. "I couldn't wait," he said.

Even Ms. Rooney was rushing.

She was calling people's names for attendance. Richard sat down at his desk.

He didn't take his jacket off. They would be getting on the bus any minute.

He looked around. Jill and Emily weren't there. He hoped they weren't absent.

He hoped the dog hadn't gotten out.

He wished he were absent.

He didn't want to find out what had happened to Drake Evans. It was all his fault.

He leaned forward. "Matthew?" he asked.

Matthew wiped some crumbs off his mouth. "That was the best," he said.

"What about Drake Evans?" Richard asked.

"Did anyone see Emily this morning?" asked Ms. Rooney. "Or Jill?"

Richard shook his head. He thought about the dog.

"Look out the window," Ms. Rooney told Dawn.

Richard tapped Matthew on the back. "Did you give Drake his homework?"

Matthew shook his head. "No. I gave it to his mother."

Just then Emily and Jill rushed into the room.

"I was getting worried," said Ms. Rooney a little crossly. "Where were you?"

Emily took a deep breath. "There's a big dog . . ."

"I knew it," Richard said.

Mrs. Gates popped her head in the door. "The bus is here," she said. "Let's go."

Richard stood up. He could see his old class walking past behind Mrs. Gates.

He didn't see Drake Evans, though.

"The dog was barking and jumping," Jill said.

Maybe something had happened to Drake.

Something terrible.

"The dog didn't bite you, did he?" asked Ms. Rooney.

Jill shook her head. "She wanted to play. That's what the man who owned her said."

"We'd better line up," said Ms. Rooney.

67

Everyone went to the side of the room.

Jill was still talking. "That dog is going to have puppies," she said. "And the man is going to give me one."

"Lucky," said Matthew.

"Yes," said Jill. "I'm going to name it Tyran-nosaurus."

The class went into the hall.

They passed the picture of James K. Polk.

"Why were you late?" Richard asked.

Emily grinned. "The dog's name is Mamie."

"Funny name for a dog," Richard said.

"Funny name for Mrs. Paris," Matthew said. "It starts with *M*."

Emily shook her head. "No good. We stopped to ask her."

"That's why we were late," Jill said.

Ms. Rooney opened the big brown door.

The class started down the path.

Richard went to the end of the line.

He hid behind the door. Maybe he could miss the bus.

Matthew looked back. "Hurry up, Beast," he yelled.

Ms. Rooney looked back too.

"Richard Best," she said. "This is no time to dillydally."

Richard hurried down the front path.

"Hurry," Matthew said again. "Don't you want to be seat partners with me?"

Ahead of them Emily climbed up the big steps of the bus. "Yikes," she yelled. "Where's my Christmas purse? The red one with the green zipper?"

Emily dashed back toward the big brown doors.

Alex climbed on the bus. Then Jill. Then Matthew. Then it was Richard's turn.

Andrew Bock from his old class yelled, "Hey, it's Beast. Hi."

"Hi," Richard mumbled. Then he looked up.

Drake Evans was sitting in the middle of the bus.

"Am I glad to see you," Richard said.

Drake looked surprised. "Hi," he said.

70

"Were you very sick?" Richard asked.

Drake shook his head. "No. I had an upset stomach."

"Move along," Ms. Rooney said.

Richard walked past Drake. He took a seat next to Matthew. He leaned forward. "Did you have blisters?"

"Are you crazy?" Drake asked.

"Are you going to move away?" Richard asked.

"You're crazy," Drake said. "I knew it."

Richard sat back. "I don't think that ruler thing worked," he told Matthew.

Emily raced back onto the bus. She sat down behind Richard, next to Dawn. "Whew," she said. "I thought my Christmas purse was lost. It was on the floor, though."

"Everything gets lost around here," Dawn said. "My ruler was lost for a week. Sometimes Jim, the custodian, puts things in the wrong desks."

Richard looked at Matthew. Then he knelt up

71

on the seat. "You're not D.T.," he told Dawn. "You're D.B."

"D.T.," Dawn said. "Dawn Tiffanie."

Richard looked out the window.

He thought about a dinosaur. The dinosaur didn't have a ruler in his paw anymore.

It was a good thing, Richard thought.

He was glad his wishes didn't come true.

The bus began to move. It turned the corner. It passed the A&P store.

In the window were stacks of candy bars. The sign said:

MINNIE'S MINT BARS

Minnie, thought Richard. *M*. Maybe Mrs. Paris's name was Minnie.

In front of him Drake turned around. He made a beast face at Richard.

Richard grinned. "Ruff-a-roo," he said.

E.G. Sherburne School